I keep going, even when things are hard

I am thankful for today

Today I choose happiness

I trust myself and my instincts

Book by Elizabeth Cole

Copyright © 2022 by Go2Publish LLC - All rights reserved

No part of this publication or the information in it may be quoted from or reproduced in any form by means such as printing, scanning, photocopying or otherwise without prior written permission of the copyright holder.
For permissions contact: go2publish.office@gmail.com

Disclaimer and Terms of Use:
The author and the publisher do not hold any responsibility for errors, omissions or contrary interpretation of the subject matter herein.
This book is presented solely for motivational and informational purposes only

Printed in China

ELIZABETH COLE

MINDFULNESS
MAKES ME STRONGER

This book belongs to

....

....

Down in the park, all the children were running around,
except for little Nick, who was sitting on the ground.
He was feeling sad and cranky, his day was pretty grim.
Nick was missing all the fun happening around him.

He didn't see the rainbow that appeared after the rain,
or the white trail in the sky made by a passing plane.
He didn't hear the ice cream van when it parked on the street,
so he missed the chance to buy his favorite frosty treat.

Nick's dad asked, "Buddy, is there something wrong?
It seems you've been in a bad mood all day long."

"Yesterday, my history test didn't go well at school.
I was also scared of the dentist, and it wasn't cool.
Lisa asked me to her birthday party, and ... I like her a lot.
And tomorrow is my game. I'm worried I'll miss a shot."

Nick's dad smiled. "Listen carefully to what I have to say. You can't change the events that happened yesterday. Instead, learn from the past and do what it takes to not keep repeating the same old mistakes."

"And don't worry about the things that haven't happened yet.
You could miss all the nice moments, which you might regret.
Instead, think about what you can change right away.
This will help you make your future better every day."

"Enjoy the present moments, those that are happening right now."
"But how do I get rid of these troubling thoughts? How? How? How?"

"Practice mindfulness. Let's start with your breathing power. Take a deep breath through your nose like you are smelling a flower."

"Think of all your big feelings that are too hard to handle.
Blow them out of your lungs like you are blowing out a candle."

"Wow! I feel better," Nick said with a twinkle in his eyes.
His father was glad. "Wait till you see our next exercise!"
"Jump up high in the air … now do it a little bit more."
Nick started jumping higher than he had ever jumped before.

"Now, put your hand over your heart and feel your heartbeat." Nick could feel the energy flowing from his head to his feet.

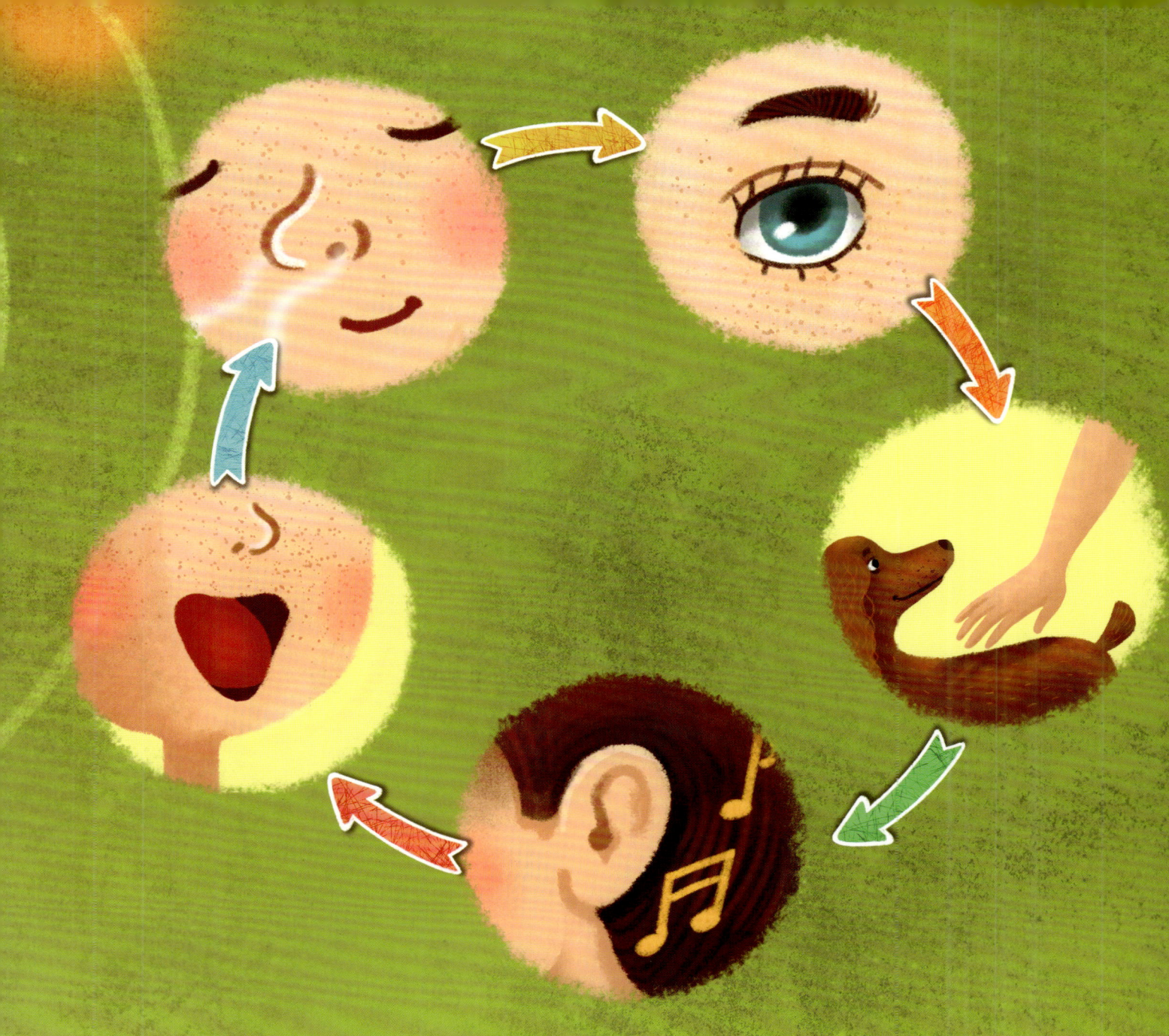

"You should pay attention to your five senses as well. Now, tell me what you see, touch, hear, taste, and smell."

"I see shapes in the clouds and hear rustling in the trees.
I smell fragrant flowers and feel the touch of the breeze."
Nick's dad picked a berry that had ripened under the sun.
"Mmm, dad, it's so delicious. May I have another one?"

Nick began to enjoy nature the way he'd never seen it before.
"Wow! Being mindful is cool and opens a whole new door."
Little Nick had replaced the frown with a smile on his face.
He now realized that the Earth was a beautiful place.

From crashing waves and squishy sand between his wiggly toes,
to the smell of fresh pastries and cookies teasing his tiny nose.
Nick was grateful for all the little things that make up his days,
from cuddles with his puppy to the warmth of the sun's rays.

He was making memories from what he saw, felt, and heard,
and he was glad to be present for his little sister's first word.
All his worried thoughts were easily driven away;
Nick began to change the things he could that day.

He started helping people paint their days in softer hues;
because being mindful means being kind to others too.

"I am helpful. I am strong. I can do it because I'm smart. I am kind, and a lot of kindness lives inside my heart."

"I appreciate others and the things that fill me with glee.
I believe in myself, and that is why I like to be ME."
The present is the place Nick has decided to live.
He enjoys every moment and all it has to give.

Finally, Nick is calm and his mind is bright and clear;
he has found true happiness in the Now and Here.
He no longer worries or is absent like he had been.
"Mindfulness makes me stronger," Nick says with a grin.

TRY THIS "WARRIOR POSE" EXERCISE TO FEEL CONFIDENT AND CONCENTRATED

- Stand up tall with your feet wide apart.
- Turn your right toes out and press your left heel away.
- Bend your right knee deeply, stretch your arms out at shoulder height and make like a surfer.
- Hang twenty seconds few relaxed breaths, feeling the strength of your body.
- Then shake out your legs and try it out on the other side.

Please go here to get your bonus coloring page for FREE

Dear Reader,

Thank you for purchasing my book!
This is the fifth story about Nick's adventures in the "World of Kids' Emotions" series.
Its purpose is to introduce children to the concept of mindfulness and help them
to regain joy and calmness of the mind.

I receive many positive reviews on my previous books and I hope you enjoyed this one too!
As always, a special gratitude goes for my young readers: your feedback and kindness
are of utmost importance and inspire me all the time!

I am very much motivated to continue Nick's adventures! So, I would like to ask you:
what kind of topic would you like to see in my next book?
Please, feel free to send me all and any thoughts and ideas. I am so excited to hear back from you!
You can write me at elizabethcole.author@gmail.com or visit www.ecole-author.com

I would also greatly appreciate it if you could review my book.
Here is the link to "Mindfulness Makes Me Stronger" on Amazon:

With love,
Elizabeth Cole